The Gift

My Journey of Singlehood

Yasmin Whirl

Published by
Our Written Lives, LLC

Our Written Lives, LLC provides publishing services for authors in various educational, religious, and human service organizations. For information, visit www.OurWrittenLives.com.

Library of Congress Cataloging-in-Publication Data
Whirl, Yasmin
The Gift: My Journey of Singlehood
Library of Congress Control Number: 2018957171
ISBN: (paperback) 978-1-942923-36-7

Scripture quotations from multiple Bible versions, as cited in-text.

Contents

Dedication

I dedicate this book to every single person on this planet who needs a boost to continue to pursue life no matter what it brings.

I dedicate this book to every heart that has been broken, and to every heart that God put back together.

I dedicate this book to every person that realizes that life can be complete without a husband or wife.

I dedicate this book to every person who desires marriage, and I dedicate this book to every person who wants no marriage at all.

I hear you loud and clear. The best is here, and life just got better!

Love,

Yasmin

According to the United States Census Bureau (2017), 110.6 million people 18 and older are unmarried in the United States of America. 63.5 percent have never been married, 53.2 percent are women, and 46.8 percent are men.

Acknowledgments

I want to thank God for making me just the way I am. I love to write. I've got a movie in me next. Watch out!

I want to thank Evangelist Lucy Rozier who confirmed years ago that there was book inside of me. Thank you for pushing me when I did not want to pick up a pen at all. You saw something in the spirit realm and you were not afraid to push as a sister in Christ.

I thank every man and woman who has poured into my life spiritually and educationally.

I thank my parents and family who always give me their blessings when I have a new idea or dream to pursue.

I thank my 9-year-old niece who asks from time to time, "Tee-Tee! When are you going to get married? Tee-Tee, when are you going to get a boyfriend?" I love her humor, and she is so serious when she asks!

Introduction

I started this book about three years ago but stopped before I finished. Last year, I picked it back up and started writing again. I saved about fifteen pages on my laptop before I had a new hard drive installed and lost all my original documents. I searched and searched, but could not find the beginning stages of my book anywhere.

Apparently, God wanted me to start all the way over, so that is what I did. I began to rewind my mind to the beginning of my journey of singleness. As I started to write, it was painful. I looked back at my life and how my heart had been broken, and how I had endured being single for—are you ready—20 years!

Why was it painful for me to look back on my life? There were still some areas God needed to do a healing work in. When my journey of singleness began, I hated it. I really thought my life was upside down. I was a church girl. I did the "right thing" most of the time. I kept my legs closed and had no night caps. Yeah, I went there.

I looked fresh when I went out and was cute most of the time. I went to college, and earned a degree. I went to graduate school and earned another two degrees. I built a house and bought a vehicle. I started a stable career in public education.

But, I still had no man in my life!

Fast forward . . . To be honest, I forgot about my singleness for a long time. I stayed busy with work, church, community service, and family functions. One day, after things slowed down a bit, I was like, "Hummm! Where's my Boo at?"

I looked around. I looked under the bed. I looked in my closet. I even looked in the toilet. I was like, "Wow! I am really still single! OMG! God, what's up? Where You be? I need You to handle this—quick!"

Fast forward again . . . About seven years ago, I received an authentic revelation that changed my entire perspective about being single. Singlehood was and is a gift! Yep! Singleness is a packaged gift from God—with no strings attached. A gift that could ultimately lead to marriage, if that is your desire.

Everybody does not want to be a wife or a husband. Some people are comfortable with dating or being a THOT. (If you don't know what a THOT is, look it up online in the Urban Dictionary.) Did I just say THOT? Yeah, I did! Well, it's not okay to be a THOT, but it is fine to be single and not desire marriage.

I have learned to cherish and appreciate the single life. I am so grateful God chose me to be single. The gift of singleness is not for everyone. I had to learn to take my eyes off of everyone else, and focus on what God was doing in my life. That's when I began to enjoy the journey of being single!

Welcome to my story, *The Gift: My Journey of Singlehood*.

A Season of Singleness

Chapter 1

I grew up in a Christian home, the oldest of two sisters. I was in the first grade when I had my first boyfriend. Yep! Even at six-years-old, I was working it—slaying it with my pigtails, bangs, and my pretty, Kool-Aid smile!

I lived in a tiny, rural town in Georgia called Toomsboro. There was nothing to do but to go to school and to church, and to do housework. That was it. Thankfully, that was all I needed at the time. My family—aunts, uncles, cousins, and grandparents, all of 'em—went to church ALL of the time.

Church was my second home. I did not quite understand it then, but as I look back, I am so grateful for the way I was raised. "Train up a child in the way he should go, and when he is old he will not depart from it" (Proverbs 22:6 NKJV).

I sang in the choir, attended Sunday School and Summer Vacation Bible School, went to weekly church services, Gospel sings, and big camp meetings. Let's not forget Bible study and prayer meetings. Oh, how could I forget? There was also Watch Night Service—where we prayed each New Year in! That was my life.

Though church was a big part of the way I was raised, I had balance with my involvement in my school's music program, marching band, and concert band. Music was my passion and outlet. I played the clarinet, the bells, and was the Drum Major all four years of high school. I even played in concert band while in college for four years.

I never really thought about it until I started writing this book, but growing up I always had a man! From elementary school to middle school, from middle school to high school, and from high school to college, I always had a boyfriend. Hey, that is just how it went! A boy would like me, and I would like him, so we would become girlfriend and boyfriend.

During the early years of my life, I thought about getting married one day, but then I would think to myself, *"That will happen after college."*

College came and I continued to date. Everything was set for me to be married on my timeline, at least that is what I thought! Little did I know, God had a different plan. His plan is always better. Trust me, I know from personal experience.

My first month in college, I discovered a newfound depth in my relationship with God. Even though I grew up in church, I honestly feel I had my salvation experience at age 18. Thank God! It was perfect timing! Growing in my knowledge of who God was and what it meant to live for Him was life changing. I had desired Christ for a very long time, but it took me 18 years to find Him for myself.

I had the typical "college experience" at the same time as I was growing in my faith. I went to college parties, experienced a full social schedule, sorority life, going to college basketball games, hanging out in the student center, and—oh, yeah—going to class. College was real, life was real, and Jesus was too!

I started feeling convicted over some of the activities and behaviors I was exposed to during that first year of college. I did not want to compromise my faith. When I commit to something I am all the way in! I had fun in college, but I did not engage in some things. At times, I earned respect for my choice to live for God. Other times, I was mocked, but I had to let it all roll off my back and keep moving.

I finally made it to my senior year of college, and about two weeks before graduation, the guy I was dating broke off our relationship. What perfect timing!

"Thanks for the early graduation gift!" I thought sarcastically. I dried my tears and focused on final exams

and the last few days of classes. I was about to graduate with my undergraduate degree!

After graduation, I went back home to Toomsboro. I needed a vehicle and some money. I needed a job! As I was job searching, the full pain of the breakup finally hit me. What did my ex-boo just do? My heart broke.

I prayed my way through the grief. As I said, when I commit to something, I am all in. When I love, I love, and breakups hurt. Finally, the pain began to lessen and my heart began to heal.

Back then, I might not have been too happy about that break-up, but today I hold no animosity toward anyone who hurt me. I gave that pain to God a long time ago. As I write, I am giving you the blunt truth of how it felt back then, but now, I look back and am thankful! The singer Travis Greene reminds us that God is intentional. He does everything for our good. The Bible tells us that too! Well, back to my story . . .

Throughout that time, my relationship with God deepened and I began hearing the voice of the Holy Spirit! Yeah, God really does speak to us! I had to grow to a place of spiritual maturity to hear Him. Wow! He spoke to me! He was guiding my footsteps and I was loving my journey. I wanted my life to please Him.

I had a hunger for God that I could not explain. Was I crazy? I wanted to be in His presence and read His

Word! Yes, at the ripe age of 22, I would rather spend time with God than go to a nightclub! Those worldly adventures never grasped my attention. Trust me, I still had my battles. I was a normal young woman. I liked to have fun and I loved men!

At times, I would think, *"I am twenty-two with a college degree and no husband, no boo, no boyfriend! Oh, well! One day, he will come."* I let loneliness roll off my back and I kept moving forward and working hard.

"Living in the past will get you nowhere," I'd say to myself. *"Learn from it and keep it moving."*

I did move on. I landed a job in public education and started working full-time. Life happened, and I began to evolve into a virtuous woman. I had my scars, wounds, and mistakes, but I owned them all.

During my twenties, my mind really was not on marriage, but I knew I wanted the company of a male. I told myself, *"My man will come before I reach thirty."* I was so sure of that!

I dated a few different men, but it just did not work out. As a young adult, my dating relationships continued to go sour, and I started questioning God about it.

"God, hello! What's up? Was it me? Was it him? Was it us? Where You be?!

"You will give me the desires of my heart, right? Can You hear me now? Do I need an Uber driver to escort me

to Heaven so we can chat? Do you need Wi-Fi so we can Facetime?"

I don't know about you, but I have to be transparent and let it all hang out when I talk with the Lord! I have always been like that. I love my relationship with God and how I can be real, and myself before Him. I love how He loves me.

I reverence our Lord and Savior Jesus Christ, and honor Him. God created me to be me, so why should I trip and act all hard? If I'm hurt, I'm hurt! If I'm upset, I'm upset! If I'm free, I'm free! If I'm delivered, I'm delivered! I am going to be real and open my heart to the Lord—no matter if I'm happy or sad, or if things are going my way or not.

Life can be disappointing and frustrating, but God Almighty has created an expected end for us all. He already knows my future and your future and has set it in motion in the spirit world. As we believe in the Lord, and yield ourselves to Him, His plan will manifest. But what do we do if blessings do not manifest when we want them to? I do not have all of the answers, but I know this: we must wait on God and trust Him!

God gave me this gift of singlehood. I've learned to walk out the gift of singlehood in the Lord. I pray you catch what I am releasing in the spirit. Fully accept the gift God has given you, own it, and walk it out.

How do you walk it out? Hold your head high! If someone dumped you, God has someone better for you. If your boyfriend slept with someone else, God has someone better for you—yes, I went there!

Life is real and sometimes it gives you sour lemons. If your relationship ended and you are hurt, that was not the relationship for you. Sure, sometimes reconciliation happens, but sometimes it does not, and it is not for us to wait around for a potential reconciliation. Let sour lemons create momentum for you to grow, stretch, and build your testimony. Find freedom today!

Scripture Moment

Trust God from the bottom of your heart;
don't try to figure out everything on your own.
Listen for God's voice in everything you do,
everywhere you go;
He's the one who will keep you on track.
Proverbs 3: 5-7 MSG

Ministry Moment
A Purpose for Your Uncomfortable Season

Life evolves gradually in seasons, months, times, cycles, and growth spurts. There is a time for every season of life (Ecclesiastes 3:1), even the uncomfortable seasons. In this journey of life, we will all experience uncomfortable seasons.

Uncomfortable. It's a word none of us like. It is the feeling of slight pain or discomfort. Irritated, distressed, disagreeable, hard, awkward, and annoying are all synonyms of the word uncomfortable. We don't welcome or celebrate uncomfortable seasons; we often want to run from them! We don't put our uncomfortable seasons on our spiritual resumes or testify about them. Uncomfortable seasons are not pleasant to the flesh, but are necessary for advancement, promotion, development, and to increase God's kingdom.

Seasons of discomfort will come, have their way, and do what they need to do in you. Then one day you will wake up and realize the season is over. The season of singleness can be an uncomfortable season, but it can also be a season where God stretches, strengthens, and stabilizes you. Your season of singleness won't last forever; it's important to make the most of it while it is here.

About three years ago, I decided to change my eating habits. I had not received a negative report from the doctor, but I was suffering from indigestion, stomach aches, and excessive flatulence. I asked the Lord, "What is going on in my body?" God told me I needed to change my eating habits.

I did not have the energy I wanted and knew I could experience. I stopped eating pork. I stopped eating too much fast food. I began eating more fruit and vegetables and drinking water. Since then, I have lost 10 pounds and I feel great! It was a rough go, at first, and I had to deny my flesh, but the results were worth it! I had to face my uncomfortable season to enter into a season full of energy and life!

No matter how content or happy you are with your life, at some point you will be hit with an uncomfortable season that will not feel right. Uncomfortable seasons will catch you totally off guard. Your uncomfortable season might be being single, or being a single parent. You might find yourself divorced and wondering how to bounce back, or facing a sickness that doesn't seem to go away.

God designed your uncomfortable season to squeeze out the oil of His Spirit that is in you. Spiritual oil symbolizes the Holy Spirit and the presence of Almighty God. In the natural, we use oil to reduce friction and clean engines. In the spiritual realm, God uses the oil of His Spirit to make you into a well-running purposed, productive part of the body of Christ. The oil of the Lord destroys the heavy yoke of friction in your mind and personality.

There is oil in you that people need! You cannot rush the uncomfortable season God has ordained to produce His oil in you. You cannot slow it down. God knows what He has designed you for, and He has already pre-qualified you for the victory! Let me say that again! You are pre-qualified for victory! This season of discomfort is just that—a season. It will pass, and you will be ready to move forward into the next season.

<u>Disclaimer #1</u>: Sometimes our uncomfortable seasons are a direct result of our own decisions. If you are guilty, you are just guilty. Own it. Be bold and be true. Face the consequences of your decisions. Turn to God's mercy and grace. Allow God to use this season to give you a tune-up.

<u>Disclaimer #2</u>: Even if your uncomfortable season is a result of your poor choices, it still often helps God's purpose for your life. Uncomfortable seasons can lead you to focus on God. Uncomfortable seasons can lead you to totally surrender all to the Lord! What the enemy means for evil in your life, the Lord will use for His good purpose.

Read Daniel 1:16-20, and Daniel 3:17 and 26.

Daniel, a leader in Old Testament, found himself in an uncomfortable season. His faith was tested when King Nebuchadnezzar exiled him from Jerusalem to Babylon. Daniel lived a righteous life, but it was the will of God for him to face captivity in a strange land. Daniel was taken to a foreign country and had to learn a new culture. During that time, he maintained his faith and triumphed. He rose to stewardship in the palace, and God used him mightily.

Daniel had the opportunity to find some physical comfort in the palace, but it would require him to compromise his faith. Instead, he chose to remain in a season of discomfort and refused to eat the King's delicacies. He ate vegetables and drank water as a way to keep himself separate and holy unto the Lord. This is where we get the idea of the Daniel Fast that many believers participate in throughout the year to refocus and dedicate themselves to the Lord.

Jesus, our Lord and Savior of the world, found Himself in an uncomfortable season too. His faith was tested while He was on assignment as Messiah, God's lamb of sacrifice for the transgression of the world's sins. Jesus completed His assignment. He focused on His position and His purpose, even though it was very uncomfortable. He was not moved. He stood on the strength of almighty God. He did not give in or give up.

Read the following scriptures, which depict His position and stance as King in a world that hated him: John 6:38, Romans 3:25 and Hebrews 10:12.

Read John 4:5-17.

The woman at the well was in an uncomfortable season. She had many husbands, but God saw her for who she was. He looked pass her marital status. He saw her heart and was willing to purify it into gold. Jesus came to give the woman at the well a new life in Him. He passed through Samaria as He traveled on His journey. He stopped at the well for a drink of water, but instead offered a Samaritan woman water that would quench her spiritual thirst in her uncomfortable season.

Jesus will rescue you in your uncomfortable season too. Nothing surprises God. He declares the end from the beginning. He already has a plan for your end. Just align with Him. He will meet you in your uncomfortable season and give you rest, peace, and a mind to make a change.

He will meet you in your uncomfortable season and give you a kingdom platform to proclaim His victorious power. God designed the uncomfortable season to bring you spiritual fruit, revelation knowledge, and kingdom principles. Let your uncomfortable season work for you.

The purpose of the uncomfortable season is to bring forth the fruit of the Spirit.

Read Galatians 5:1, 22-23.

The fruit of the Spirit is the manifestation of a Christ transformed life. Spiritual fruit will help us keep a clear mind, stay focused, and have a heart full of love for God's people. The Fruit of the Spirit are attributes Christians should embody and live out.

The purpose of the uncomfortable season is to bring forth revelation knowledge.

Read Proverbs 2:6 and Proverbs 18:15.

When you are in the middle of a battle between your flesh and your spirit, draw close to the Word of God. The Word will give you power, strength, a sound mind, and peace that every part of your life, even the uncomfortable ones, are working for your good.

Grab hold of knowledge and make it useful. Knowledge is only good if we apply it. How do you apply it? Add knowledge into your day to day activities. Ask yourself, "What would Jesus have me to do? Should I make this decision? Will God get the glory?" Go to the Word of God and make sure it aligns with the plan and vision God has for you.

The purpose of the uncomfortable season is to bring forth kingdom principles.

Read I Corinthians 4:20.

The kingdom of God is full of empowering resources that are relevant, will sustain you, and will bring you out of your uncomfortable season. When you feel that you cannot go on, I promise you—you can! Tap into your inner man and your inner strength in the Lord.

There are seeds of God's wisdom and knowledge planted deep within you. Find some time to meditate on God's Truth. Get into God's Word. Allow the rain of the Holy Spirit to water those seeds in you.

Give yourself time, and allow God to do a work in your uncomfortable season. You will grow and yield fruit. Allow His authority to rise up in you. Put on the mind of Christ.

Pen Moment

Reflect back to your younger years, from the time you were 5-years-old to 25-years-old. As you think back, if anything triggers any thought of pain, frustration, or alienation write it down in your journal. Ask God to purge it from your heart.

Allow God to take you through an uncomfortable season of cleaning up the soil of garden of your soul, so He can grow something new in you. Let Him clean you up spiritually the way a hot shower with soap cleans the grime and dirt off the crevices of your skin. God has a new and fresh beginning waiting for you now.

Prayer Moment

Eternal God our Father, you are King and Savior of this world. You are the survival kit that completes my world and sets it in motion.

Heal me of any pain from my past and current state of living. May I refrain from carrying my past into my future, unless it is as a testimony only. My past was only designed to carry me through. It has happened and it can no longer haunt me.

I am free of the shame, embarrassment, and any unanswered questions that still linger. I am moving forward. I am progressing. I am accelerating in what You, God, have for me.

God, conceal the enemy of doubt, anxiety, and discouragement. I speak life into the atmosphere and declare change for the better. I am more than a conqueror and I have been given a new set of lenses to view my life through. I anticipate what you have for me. Just for me.

Amen.

Total Release and Surrender

Chapter 2

Every ten years or so, I have a big pow-wow with the Lord. He always wins. You may feel like you cannot question God, but I am wired full of questions for the Creator!

He created me with a curious mind. I reverence Him, as I ask my questions, and, you know, He gives such revelation! It blows my mind as He reveals His Word and it comes alive.

When I was about 30-years-old, I had a very significant moment with the Lord one morning in my one-bedroom apartment. I was at a breaking point in my life.

It was Saturday morning, and I could hear the birds chirping and the dogs barking as I begin to talk with God. It was my regular routine morning devotion time, but that day was different. I was full of emotion, unanswered questions, and desires that had not been fulfilled. Everything seemed to hit me at once.

Have you had moments like that? We all do and its normal. As a certified school counselor, I have to say that if you have strong emotions more than three days a week, you need to seek professional help, as you may be experiencing the onset of depression.

I stopped my routine prayer and looked up at the ceiling. "God, why am I not married?" I asked. My question was the precursor to Tyler Perry's movie, *Why did I get Married?*

I waited, but God said nothing.

"God, I humble myself and I reverence You as Abba, but Your daughter has got some questions and I really need some answers. I am Your vessel. You created me 30 years ago. If marriage is for me, then I must wait! If marriage is not for me, then I must be content with it and move on."

I continued to pray, and again and again, I asked, "God, why am I not married?"

I waited, and God still said nothing.

Again, I asked, "God why am I not married?"

I took a deep breath and boldly said, "I am not going anywhere until you answer. I need some answers today!"

I felt a release in the spirit and God begin to speak as I emptied myself unto Him. All the tears, toxins, pain, and misery—I gave it to him. He filled me up with his love, tender mercies, joy, and revelation. It was total surrender.

I guess you are wondering what He said? Suspense! Suspense!

God began to reveal His plan for me, and confirmed in my spirit that marriage was for me!

"Okay! Thank You, God!" I said with enthusiastic relief, but then He continued.

He said marriage was for me, but not for now.

"OOOOOOKKKKKKKKKKKKKKAAAYYYY! But why not now?" Me and my big mouth cried again.

"It is in your future, but You must trust me. Trust me and I will take you on a journey," God said.

I dropped my head, not in shame, but in total surrender.

"Okay, God! Okay, Jehovah! Okay, King of Kings! Okay, Rose of Sharon! You want me, You got me! You want all of me? Here You go! Here I am! Do whatever You want to do, and I will live and exalt Your name in all I do! While You are taking me on this truth journey, teach me all about You, and how to be a wife and a mother. Whatever You say to do, I will do it!"

The Spirit of the Lord lifted my heart, and I was free! He freed me from pain and agony. I had His assurance, and I trusted Him with my life!

That day, I began a brand new, exciting journey of singlehood. I decided to surrender my will to the will of God. Before that day, I was fighting a fight I would never win because God's will for me was singleness, and I was pursuing relationships—the opposite direction of where God wanted me. My choices were causing an inner collision between my flesh and God's Spirit.

It's easy for an internal clash to happen in any area of our lives. We have to yield to what God has for us in the current time and season. Just yield. It takes some time, but if I can do it, I know you can.

I began to embrace every day. I began to research living a life of being single. I began to attend singles conferences. I sought out knowledge from a plethora of areas: The Holy Bible, the newspaper, the Internet, YouTube . . . I was seeking wisdom from others who had walked this path.

I began to order books, read, and learn all I could about being single. On my journey, the Holy Spirit let me know what I needed to receive and what I needed to dump from what I read. The Holy Spirit is intelligent and does not play when it comes to His children.

I even started a singles ministry at my church. Guess what? All the singles that were in my group are all married now! I am so happy for them and celebrate what God has done in their lives! My journey of singlehood is different from others, but I trust God, and am still trusting Him every step of the way.

I have dated on my journey, but the relationships never evolved into any lasting commitments. I always kept God at the center of my relationships. He is so unique and always honest with me. I would meet guys and the Holy Spirit would be like, "You know that's not your husband . . ."

"Thanks a lot, God. I really dig him! He's hot and he's a keeper!"

"You are right, but he is not yours!" God would say back to me.

I am telling you, when you commune with God, He will reveal the truth. You better be ready! God would reveal Himself to me through everything I went through.

Each time a relationship would end, and the ex-boyfriend would marry someone else, I would have to admit the truth: "God, You were right!"

When I was in my second or third year of college, I met a guy through a mutual friend that introduced us. We met in the college cafeteria. He was so fly, but he was also so far from the Kingdom of God.

I thought I would give it a try to see where it went. The guy treated me like royalty and was kind. I was his woman and he was my man. He respected my wishes and knew I was a church girl, but he would spend his nights working or at the club partying.

We did not share the same lifestyle. He never would attend church with me. Can people change? Yes. Am I passing judgment? No! It just is what it is. I had to end the relationship and the guy wanted to know why.

"I been faithful to you and I've been straight with you. We are good together," he said.

And we were good together.

I pulled out my Bible and reminded him of the God I represented. We were unequally yoked. I wanted more than a thrill. I wanted spiritual leadership and a bond of faith. That man could not provide it.

He understood and wished me well. From the day I ended that relationship, my spirit was no longer quenched. If the person you are dating cannot go with you to the next level in God, you need to cut them loose! That's the truth!

As you grow in the things of God, and as you surrender more to him, you will soon realize your walk is more important than appeasing your flesh. If a relationship does not glorify the King, or if it vexes your spirit, cut it loose!

Scripture Moment

But without faith it is impossible to [walk with God and] please Him, for whoever comes [near] to God must [necessarily] believe that God exists and that He rewards those who [earnestly and diligently] seek Him.

Hebrews 11:6 (Amplified Bible)

Ministry Moment
My End Will Be GOOD!

Read Luke Chapter 5.

The story opens with Jesus teaching and preaching on the shore of the Sea of Galilee, also called the Lake of Gennesaret. The Sea of Galilee was the largest freshwater lake in Israel. It was thirteen miles long and seven miles wide. The water was best known for fishing, trade, and its sudden, violent storms.

Jesus had performed many miracles around the city of Galilee. He was always on point and exercised His gift of healing with excellence. This chapter gives us a close look at what Jesus does best—being God and completing His assignment.

Jesus knew who He was—great, mighty, and victorious. His mindset tapped into the spiritual realm and He was able to release a word of healing in a time when He experienced both the rejection and the love of many.

The crowds pressed in upon Jesus. Maybe He needed a platform to speak to the entire crowd, instead of just a few who wanted His direct attention. That's when He saw two empty boats in the water. Jesus saw the empty place as useful. He stepped into one of the boats and continued to teach.

Normally, a fishing boat on the shore would be full of fish, but these boats were empty. The fishermen had given up. Maybe they were standing in the shallow waters washing their nets when Jesus took over the boat. Maybe they were part of the crowd that stood listening to Him teach.

Jesus finished teaching and turned to Simon, one of the fishermen. "Launch into the deep and let down your net," He commanded.

Nobody had told Jesus what was going on. Nobody had posted a pic or live video on Snapchat, Facebook, or Twitter. Jesus didn't know they had tried fishing all night long and nothing was working.

Simon turned to Jesus with a perplexed look on his face. "Master, we have been out here all night long and have nothing."

The men had already done their best. They felt like there was nothing left to do but clean the nets and go home. But they made a decision to try one more time, obeying Jesus even though it seemed hopeless.

They released what was in their hand. They put their thought process aside and followed the Lord's specific instructions. It was a simple directive, but on the opposite side of the boat. It didn't make sense according to their understanding of the way the underwater world worked, but their obedient surrender produced unfathomable results.

"And when they had this done, they inclosed a great multitude of fishes: and their net brake. And they beckoned unto [their] partners, which were in the other ship, that they should come and help them. And they came, and filled both the ships, so that they began to sink." (Luke 5:6-7 KJV).

The end of their story was nothing like their beginning. Neither is yours. Your end will be greater than your beginning. What have you been scratching your head about lately? What have you been toiling with? What is bothering you? What has a hold of you that takes you further away from the Father?

God wants to step into the empty places of your life. He sees something significant and useful in your emptiness. Your empty place may feel dry and dead, but God sees life. Your relationship may seem hopeless, but God sees restoration.

If the boats had been full of fish, Jesus wouldn't have been able to use the boat as a platform to teach the people. God had every intention of providing for the fishermen before the day was over, but if the blessing had come too soon, they would have missed out on a part of their God-intended purpose. Simon Peter and the other soon-to-be disciples may not have given God the glory for the miracle of the fish if they had received them before the right time.

Jesus has His eye on you. He sees and hears everything. He knows about your empty places. He sees how much you've been toiling and trying to make your life happen. He wants to perform a miracle in your life. He wants to answer your prayer. He wants to beckon you to your blessing, but you must release what is in your hand. You must release your understanding of the situation. You must let go of your ideas about how your blessing should come.

Sometimes to receive a harvest, we must first release and surrender something to God. It is human nature to try to fix the issues that arise in our lives. It is human nature to attempt to solve problems on our own, but it is supernatural to say, "God, I need you. I need Your help today. I can't do this on my own."

It is okay to release your cares to God. You do not have to carry your burden. He will make it light and weightless. Matthew 11:30 (KJV) says, "My yoke is easy and my burden is light." We can rest in Him and find confidence in any situation we face.

The word "release" means to set free from restraint or confinement. To let go. To relieve from something that confines, burdens, or oppresses. To liberate from anything that restrains or fastens.

God wants to set you free from anything that has you bound. His victory awaits us. The enemy attempts to restrain us by making our issues seem larger than what they are. But in God's presence, those issues deflate. He is enlarged in us through His Word.

God is a God of liberation and freedom. He says in John 10:10, "I am come that you may have life and have it more abundantly."

The New Living Translation puts it this way, "My purpose is to give them a rich and satisfying life."

The God's Word Translation reads, "But I came so that my sheep will have life and so that they will have everything they need."

We have to release, surrender, and set free what we are holding onto if we want to receive what God has for us.

God has given us the gifts of salvation, love, eternal life, acceptance, unmerited favor, and redemption through His blood. We are blessed! We have an assurance. Many blessings are automatic when we fully realize who we are in Christ.

We must know our position in Christ. Our position with Him allows us to take full authority in our rightful place as believers. We are conquerors, mighty warriors. Our position declares that our end is good! Our position allows the Holy Spirit that resides within us to take charge and guide us day by day. Our position ensures power and strength in times of adversity and times of success.

You are more than a woman. You are more than a man. You are a conqueror. You are an overcomer. You are a king. You are a queen. You are a prince. You are a princess. You are a catalyst for change!

You are who God says you are! God has given us the authority to receive His spiritual blessings. We are a part of God's royal priesthood. We are adopted into a kingdom of royalty!

When we fully embrace, when we fully capture, and understand who we are in God, life will change for the better. Life will evolve. Life will flourish. You will see what you can do. You will see what you can accomplish. You will see what you can achieve. With God, I feel as if I can do anything! And I believe the same for you!

When we release our plans and lives over to Christ, we will receive what He has for us! Release your seed and obtain a promise!

In the game of football, the quarterback has to release the football to his teammate on the field in order to score a touchdown. Once he releases the football and one of the players catches the ball, there is a good opportunity that they will score a touchdown.

The football is symbolic of something you have been holding on to for too long. Release that ball to the Lord—He is on your team—and receive a touchdown!

Release your net and receive your harvest!

Simon had to release what was in his hand. He had to obey and release the net and launch into the deep. He had to trust God and obey His command.

What is in our hand is not enough to pull us through the night. We have to let God take what we have so He can turn it into something greater. Let God grow through you!

Release your agenda and receive revelation knowledge!

When I lay my agenda aside and give God full reign, I receive results. I am learning to release more and more each day. It's a trust issue for me, and something I have to continually practice in my faith walk.

"God, are You really gonna handle this for me?"

"Yes, I will."

"God, are You really going to answer my prayer?"

"Yes, I will."

Often, our circumstances go against all hope, but we must make a decision to step out on faith and obey the Word of God. We must decide to try Jesus. It sounds cliché, but it works!

We triumph in victory because of the guaranteed promises of God. We are guarnteed an overflow, a harvest of a magnitude of health, wellness, wealth, prosperity, authority, and spiritual blessings.

Ephesians 1:3 (KJV) says, "Blessed be the God and Father of our Lord Jesus Christ, who hath blessed us with all spiritual blessings in heavenly places in Christ."

Isaiah 59:16 (KJV) reminds us that, "When the enemy shall come in like a flood, the Spirit of the LORD shall lift up a standard against him."

When the enemy comes in like a thief, God will lift up a defense. When the enemy comes in unannounced, God has you covered. God will lift up a standard of love, a standard of grace, a standard of protection, a standard of direction, a standard of peace.

It is yours for the receiving—simply surrender and release your life into His care!

Pen Moment

Breathe in.
Exhale.
Breathe in.
Exhale.
It's okay. God has got you. He knows just where you are at. What do you need to surrender to God?

Write down what God is asking you to release to Him. Write down what action He is asking you to take in an act of obedient faith.

Prayer Moment

Lord God,

Make me over again. I want to be an example of Your love. As I walk and live this singlehood journey, make Your plans clear to me. May my ears not be dull of hearing You in the Spirit.

In Your will is where I find hope, joy, and endurance. In Your will is where I find my future, desires, and true authentic ministry.

May my life and its outcome be what You want and what I need. I lay aside my agenda to pick up Yours. You created the end from the beginning so You already know what it will be for me. May my trust arise and my anxiety decrease.

I love you. Amen.

In the Middle

What do you do while you are in between a prayer and an answer? How do you live when you are struggling to trust God and walk by faith? How do you survive as you hold onto your promise until it unfolds? How do you keep believing when your answer has not yet manifested?

In the middle of your faith walk, your journey, and your deepest desires, live life to the utmost and find something amazing to do every day! God creates every day to be unique, and He has designed you for a purpose right in the middle of it!

Think about it. Each day of the week is different. They each have a different name, and a different number on the calendar. As each day comes and goes, you are one step closer to your destiny; just take it one day at a time.

God is not on our time schedule. He operates outside of time, and His timing is perfect. His ways are guaranteed. His process is authentic and will produce purposeful fruit.

Slow down. Slow down. Slow down.

Women, your husband will find you; I promise you that. Men, your wife will appear in your path when God says you both are ready. Of course, God gave us a brain to use and we can think for ourselves, but if you want His best and the finest He has, you better play the cards of life He has dealt you. I promise He will not disappoint you. You won't miss your spouse if you remain in God's will.

Your journey of singlehood is a part of God's process for your life. Let God repair you from your past. Let God work on you and refuel you. Singlehood is the time you have to learn how to manage you. It's a great time to learn who you are and to develop an identity.

Do you know who you are?

I'm not asking what your family, your culture, or your heritage says you are. I am asking you, who are you?

Who are you when the curtains close and the phone rings? How do you handle disappointment? How do you deal with drama? Who are you when no one is watching? Who are you when you get home from work and begin to unwind? Who are you when the sun rises early in the morning and the moon appears at night?

You need to have an answer for the other side of each question mark. If you don't have an answer, seek God to find your purpose, calling, and destiny. God has a purpose for you that is connected to Him. Stop trampling and stampeding over yourself and God to get to the marriage altar!

I battled for years to find my identity. Let me be clear, I know I am a female and a woman. I have never struggled with my gender identity, but I did struggle to find out who I was as a person. I don't know why I had to go through that stage of finding myself, but I did—more than once. I had to ask the age-old questions, "Who I am? Why I am?"

Some people identify themselves by their boyfriend, girlfriend, or spouse. Their entire identity is wrapped up in their relationship status, but a relationship is not who you are. Yes, I feel some haters with that remark, but it's the truth.

Are you waiting on a man or a woman to define your identity on this earth? Are you waiting on an event to stabilize you? Are you waiting on something from the highest Himalaya Mountain to hit you on the head and make you over?

Are you waiting on a person to take you places and make you better? If so, you need to rise up quick, fast, and in a hurry! I do not have time to wine, dine, and stroke you with an enchanting interlude to inspire you to find yourself. I have to hit you in the gut—hard. That's how I roll! I have had many days and many nights to think, ponder, and wonder. I have had many hours and minutes to search, digest, and repress. I have had many years to think about all of this, do it well, and do it again. I soon realized I had to get myself together, or I was going to waste away.

It is time for you to get yourself together and make do with what you have. Stop whining and complaining. Stop putting stupid posts on social media. Everybody knows that you are single and you want a boo. I want a boo too, but until it happens, I'm going to live on top of the world.

You may ask yourself, "Is it my fault I haven't met someone?" I used to ask myself that, until I became tired of the question floating in my head. I soon put it in the trashcan, and so should you!

After I graduated from college, over 20 years ago, I dated a guy who told me, "You do not have an identity."

I was fireball mad at him for saying that, but he was right. I had too much pride to tell him he was right. I had grown into a young blissful person, but I had boundaries and limitations all around me. I had to decide if I was going to jump in the game or stay on the sidelines.

Ask yourself these questions: What do you like? What will you engage in? Who is in your circle? Why do you do what you do? What do you want in a mate? What do you bring to the table? Are you worth it? Once you discover who you are, you have to be comfortable in your own skin.

As a mature adult you must be able to say, "No." As a mature adult you must also be able to say, "Yes."

Practice it!

"No is my final answer."

"Yes is my final answer."

"Hmm, I missed the mark. I made a mistake. I learned from it and moved on."

Respect yourself first and others will follow. Yes, I know I am far from perfect. I have my scars and wounds, but I know my Redeemer lives! I know who I am, and I am who I am. Take it or leave it. It's my world and I claim it.

Clap, baby! It's your world and you claim it as well! You must find completion in you before you find your mate. Let God complete you now; do not wait. You can stand by yourself until he or she comes. I have faith in you. I do not know you, but I believe God can make you whole and complete now. Completion is in the atmosphere now. You can ask God for it, and He will do it. We hear that all the time, but I actually believe it. I hope you will believe with me.

If you are struggling about who you are and why you are, let God arise in you and do a work. How can He do that? One day at a time, with you learning about you, how you like you, and how you appreciate you. During your days of singleness, instead of complaining and having your head down, Rise UP!

The Atlanta Falcons are not the only ones who need to RISE UP! You rise up! Clean up! Pray up! Live up! Begin to speak positive words and affirmations into the atmosphere.

Words have power. Words have value. Words have substance. Words can change your situation. Speak God's Word concerning your situation. I have learned how to open my mouth and make daily declarations. I have learned how to command my day before it breaks forth and emerges.

Every day, I declare I am rich. I declare I am made whole. I declare I am healed of any infirmity. I declare I am debt free. I declare I am made and created in the image of God. I declare my future mate is in the hand of God. I declare the courtship, relationship, and engagement are all ordained by God. I declare we shall honor God.

I declare he shall love all of these rolls and luscious thick hips! Yeah, I went there. You got to have some fun even when you are speaking with God. He likes a little humor!

I declare I already have answers and solutions to problems. I declare work shall be peaceful and not chaotic. I declare I am enjoying life!

Your declarations may not be the same as mine; that is fine. You know what your needs are. Own your needs.

Own your problems. Own your world. Own and trust that God has a plan for you. He does have a plan for you.

Hear me! He has a plan for you. He has a plan for you. He has a plan for you. He has a plan for you!

Hear me with your spiritual eyes, ears, and the Holy Ghost. Let nobody ride over what you are believing for. If they are not in agreement with you, don't share your dreams with them anymore. They are dream-killers.

God will surround you with people who will believe and push you into your destiny. Unwrap the gift of singleness God has given you. Untuck it from under your bed. Go dig into your closet and open that gift. Blow the dust off that gift. Go find it in your trunk and unwrap it.

I am thankful for my gift of singleness. When I found the gift, unwrapped it, and saw ALL that God had for me, OH, MY GOODNESS! I love my gift and treasure it.

Do I want a man? Yes, I most certainly do. Do I want to get married? Yes, I most positively do. Do I want children? Yes, I most certainly do. Do I want those labor pains . . . ? Well, I'm not so sure about that!

I've learned there is more in life than being a spouse or a parent; though those are admirable roles that have their place in society. Our family roles shape and mold us into who we are as human beings. As this earth orbits the sun, we should each have a solid identity in Christ. We must know who we are outside of any other person.

We must know our true identity. I am a person. I am a human being. I am talented. I am gifted. I am somebody. After you say, "I do," what will you have to offer?

Don't go to the altar empty. Yep, I went there again. You and I should be full. Good God, Almighty! I felt that!

In the meantime, explore, expand, and enlarge. Explore this thing call life. Expand your dimension. Enlarge your territory. Learn something new. Do something different. God created us and packed us with wisdom, gifts, and so much more!

My personal burning bush moment with God at the ripe age of 30 was getting real and more real every day. I was like, "Okay, this is real. I am still single! I love you God, but it's time to release my man!"

God was like, "No, its not!"

"Okay, God! You got me! What did I do wrong? What am I supposed to do? Should I go get me a man and tell him to marry me?" Some people do that and are miserable. They are never truly happy.

I decided to just keep living. I kept pushing. As days and nights came and went, I found truly unspeakable joy in the teeny-weeny things in life we so often take for granted. I learned to focus, or channel, my energy into other things besides having a man.

I would take myself to the movies. I would take myself out to dinner. I would take myself shopping. I would get into my car and travel. That's right! My relationship with God was getting deeper and deeper.

Was I a Jesus freak, holier than though? No, I was not. I was just a normal lady who valued herself, who loved the male specimen, but had a heart that yearned for God more.

Friday nights came. Saturday nights came. Holidays came. Months came. Years came. They all went by with no Boo. No Big Daddy! No Baby Cakes! Was I mad? Not anymore. Was I jealous of my friends who had a mate? No. Jealousy is a stupid spirit. Thankfully, I have never battled it.

I like to celebrate what others have. I celebrate couples who are dating or engaged. I celebrate couples who are married and in covenant with each other. I even pray for married couples. Yep, I do! I sow the seed and trust God will water it.

Some of you may think, "Hmmm, how she pray for married couples and she ain't married?" So glad you asked! I pray the word of God over them!

Until the scope of my destiny and desires unfold and become crystal clear, I am enjoying my gift of singlehood. For my peeps who are not in an identity crisis and know who you are, I am glad for you, but I have something for you as well. Can you become a better you? Can you work on you?

In the middle of this *thang* called singlehood, in the middle of being in the middle, in the middle of your relationship, in the middle of dating, in the middle of your life, in the middle of waiting on your answer, do not rush. Do not get anxious. Do not try to speed it up!

Do I need to go get Paul, the Apostle from the Holy Bible, to come give you a citation from one of his books in the New Testament? Do not try to slow it down or to speed it up. Own where you are right now! Take a deep breath and pray, "God, if this is where you got me, I will walk it out with fidelity."

Jill Scott, the award winning singer and songwriter, sang a song titled, *Golden*. She says to live your life like it is golden. Do it! As you do that, watch your steps. Your steps will carry you into a land overflowing with milk and honey. Ask Joshua and Caleb from the book of Numbers in the Bible.

Will you get a little scared? Yes. Will you have some bloopers? Yes. Will it be easy? No. Will you make it? Yes. Will you make it? Yes. Will you make it? Yes!

God will direct your steps and carry you into all of your desires. May the Lord God almighty enlarge your territory and expand your provision. May the Lord God shift your mindset and thinking to something of substance. Do not be small minded. Stretch. Grow. Cultivate. Gather. Produce. Germinate.

Scripture Moment

"Come to me, I will give you rest."
Matthew 11:28 NIV

Ministry Moment
Contagious Faith

Read Romans 12:3 and Hebrews 11:6.

The word contagious is often associated with something negative that you want nothing to do with. We usually use the word contagious when describing a sickness or disease that easily spreads. If something is contagious, it is highly communicable, or easy to catch.

We do not want to be in the pathway of contagious diseases. We take extra precautionary steps to prevent contagious sicknesses from spreading. When we hear the word contagious, or that something is contagious, most of us immediately go into protection mode. We do whatever we need to do to stay far, far away from whatever it is, so it will not infect us.

Epidemics of contagious diseases capture the attention of government officials at the state and local levels, and sometimes even as high up as the White House. When a problem breaks out, nothing can track it or stop it. Nature has to take its course. Once the damage is done, we assess the situation and move forward, hopefully before it becomes a pandemic.

But what if something positive was contiguous? What if our faith was contagious? What if our faith spread and was unstoppable? What if our faith was untraceable and caused a prophetic impact on this nation?

What if the words of faith we release into the spirit world, and believe God for, were to shift the very atmosphere of the world? What if our faith became a magnet and drew people to the word of the Lord? What if our faith was contagious?

Read Romans 12:3.

How much is a measure? It is not enormous, but it is also not an immeasurable tiny amount. What will you do with your measure of faith? Will you hold on to it, hoping and wishing it will grow? Do you protect it in a box, and keep it on a shelf? Do you dream about it? Or do you water it, and expose it to the light, so it will grow?

God has given each of us a measure of faith. What are you doing with your faith? Your faith won't work unless you work it.

Popular Christian speaker, Joyce Meyers said, "Faith has a language."

Pastor Martin Brock said, "Faith has a voice and it has to be activated."

Your voice or language of faith will be different than the people around you. Have you ever noticed that successful men and women have a different mind-set? They talk a different talk. They are like magnets. People are drawn to them.

Let's make a conscious decision to activate our faith! I want contagious faith that ignites something in everyone around me. I will start with activating my faith first, and you start with you! Wherever you go, let your faith go before you. Contagious faith will result in miracles, signs, and wonders for the glory of God!

Remember, the word contagious is defined as: *transmissible by direct or indirect contact, exciting similar emotions or conduct in others, or tending to spread from person to person.*

Every day, after I wake up and engage in my morning devotion, I get dressed and drive to work. I may listen to a morning show by Steve Harvey or Rickey Smiley.

Most days, I turn the radio down and just start decreeing and declaring words of faith over my day and the people I will encounter.

"I am believing God for _______. I thank God that He has already done _______."

I have made it a point to activate my day with hope, peace, solutions, and a voice that turns away wrath and anger.

As I grow in the things of God, my faith declarations have moved beyond speaking blessings for my relatives, friends, and acquaintances. I've started speaking faith over events I see on the news. I feel a spiritual release when I speak faith into the atmosphere.

I read about how Grammy award winning actor, Will Smith, and his son, Jaden, have a water company called JUST. They donate clean water to schools in Flint, Michigan. The area has not had clean water since 2014, after the state switched their water supply from Lake Huron to the Flint River. The Flint River has very high levels of lead in it, and has caused severe health damage to the people of the area.

The Smiths saw a problem, and had the faith to do something about it. They took the resources they had in their hand and took an act of faith to step in and help people in need.

You may not be able to donate clean water to a city of people, but you can do something with what you have. What are you doing with your faith? Have you ignited your faith? Or is it dormant? Have you given up, or are you using your measure of faith to its maximum capacity?

I believe in seasons of faith. I have times where my faith is stronger than other times, but I also believe in making a choice to activate my faith. I believe in momentum and achievement. I am in my early 40s, and I want to see God do more in my life and the lives of others than I have ever seen before. God has too many blessings for us to just sit down on our faith. I am determined to live my life with more decreeing and declaring.

You may say, "I don't have the time to activate my faith. I am cooking, working with my child, helping with homework . . ." I understand we all have responsibilities, and that we don't have time to waste. But you do have time to activate your faith!

You may be on the toilet or in the shower, but start believing God for something. You may be driving on the way to church or work, but you can decree something! Speak more faith into the atmosphere! Bomb-rush your soul with the fire of God. Ask Him to lite up your spirit to want more of Him.

You may say, "I am comfortable where I'm at." Okay, but what about your sister or brother, or your spouse or someone you know? They may be in need for your faith to step in and declare a word over their lives. Let's release our faith! We can do this! We can change the world. We can make invisible deposits that will yield visible returns.

Read Philippians 4:8, Romans 12:2, Matthew 21:22, II Corinthians 10:5, and Ephesians 2:8.

The mind is a spiritual battle ground. Take back the areas of your mind that the enemy has stolen! Don't sit back passively. Activate your faith! How do I release my faith? It is simple. Use your mind, your heart, and your mouth.

What are the benefits of contagious faith? Contagious faith will maximize your capacity to receive.

The definition of maximize is, "to increase or make as large as possible. To expand, amplify, or magnify."

Read John 1:16, Psalms 23:1, and Jeremiah 17:7-8.

Contagious faith will accumulate your spiritual inheritance.

The definition of accumulate is, "to gather or build in masses." God has a spiritual inheritance that is rightfully ours as His children; we don't have to earn it.

Read Proverbs 8:20-21, Titus 3:7, Colossians 1:12.

Contagious faith will empower you to live a life of abundance.

The definition of abundance is, "a large quantity, prosperous."

We can live a life flowing with milk and honey, without lack. When lack is in the house, the enemy is up to something, but God is too. Keep pressing forward in faith and allow the Holy Spirit to close loopholes and provide resources.

As the Life Application Study Bible exhorts us concerning Hebrews 1, *"Leave room for the unexplainable works God!"*

Read Luke 6:38, II Corinthians 9:8, and Psalm 37:29.

Pen Moment

Make a list of everything you are believing God for. As it comes to pass, begin to refer back to your list and check it off as you receive answers.

Prayer Moment

Lord, You are mighty. I ask You to close every trapdoor the enemy has set in my way. It will not open, but it will remain closed forever.

Lord, open doors You intend for me to walk through. As I walk through Your doors of opportunity and blessings, teach me to receive and appreciate all You have in store for me. Shield me with Your blood of protection and the breastplate of righteousness.

My feet shall step onto fertile ground and I will walk by faith. My faith will transform my world and shape and mold me into what You have created me to become.

You are the Potter; I am the clay. Make me over again in Your image. Your image beholds the beauty of the super person I am. I reach beyond the brokenness to find You, as You wrap me in Your arms.

I am ready for what You have in store for me.

Amen.

This Thing Called Dating

Chapter 4

Let's get to the heart of this chapter. You probably noticed it's called, "This Thing Called Dating." Did you pick up this book thinking it was about dating? This book is not to teach you how to catch a man or a woman, but this chapter will give you a glimpse of my personal dating journey. This book is to help you enjoy and take ownership of where you are at this very moment, and to move you to the next level.

Dating. Where do I begin? I have met some doozies in my day, I will tell you that. Some were appetizers, just that sort of quick fix. Some were entrées that were so well-done I couldn't digest them. Some were desserts, just tasty and that was it. Ha! Ha! Ha! I love my humor!

Dating . . . Where do I begin? In my early stages of dating, I would take company at my parent's house. That moved to sitting under the garage at my grandmother's house "courting," as the old folks call it. I have dated a plethora of men, from a mama's boy, to a former thug, to a cynical preacher. I've dated divorced men, and men who just needed someone to vent to. I have moved from being a sounding board, to being a main chick, to hearing a man say, "I don't want to date you no more." It hurt, but life is real! That's why we have to put on that full armor of God. The darts will come, and you will have to take some blunts, bullets, and pellets.

People will lie, and people will tell the truth. People will love you, and people will hate you. People will give to you, but people will also use you. This is real talk. Am I angry about what happened to me? No. I'm just giving it to you straight. Did it hurt when it happened? Shucks yeah—"Straight Outta Compton!" I will leave that to Ice Cube and his crew . . . This is Straight Outta Singlehood! Hello?! It is what it is!

For the next part of this chapter, I'm going to describe some guys I have dated along the way. I have changed their names, but I wanted to describe them to you and tell you what I learned from dating each one.

Guy 1

I will call him Quinton. Quinton was a college graduate and had a decent career. He was active in the church and quite handsome. He was smoking on Whirl, and I was smoking on him. We dated twice, but it didn't work either time. Each time, we mutually agreed to end it. He went on to marry someone else.

My version of the issue was that he was too busy for me. He was so caught up in work, community service, and church work, he never had time for me. Actually, he never made time for me.

My Lesson: If you want to get married you have to carve some time in your life to date. I was ready, but he was not.

Guy 2

Let me tell you about Romeo. Catch me with your bad self! Romeo was cute and hot! He liked Whirl, and I liked him. He lived in another state, but he always made time for me. We talked several days a week and he would visit once a month. We also dated twice, but it did not work. We eventually went our separate ways and I never heard from him again. He is now married and retired.

My version of what happen to our relationship was that we were in two different lanes of life. I wanted marriage, but not at that time. I was in college and very ambitious. When we dated the second time, I was ready for marriage and he was not. Apparently, we were not meant to be.

My lesson: You must be going the same direction for a dating relationship to develop into engagement and marriage.

Guy 3

Pastor Strawberry. Pastor Strawberry approached me with much poise and stamina after a church service one night. I was intrigued. He would write me letters and he called every day, but it went nowhere. I mean absolutely nowhere. I had fun while it lasted, but all he wanted to do was talk about God. Really?! We are not in heaven, and I do other things beside love Jesus!

I could not take it! I tried several times to divert the conversation in other directions, but he always came back to Jesus. He never would let his guard down and be a real person with me. I ended that fling quickly and never looked back!

My lesson: Let's have balance, people!

Guy 4

I will refer to him as Dontez. I was done on the first date, but I was open to trying something different. I wanted to give him the benefit of the doubt. Dontez was my first experience dating a mama's boy, and my last! We could not make it through a conversation without discussing his mama and what he had to do for her. Every time he wanted to go out, he wanted to take his mama along! I was done!

I am family oriented and love my family. I know dating and marriage involve family gatherings, but you cannot bring your mama on your dates!

Dontez is married now, and he is probably still talking about his mama. How did we meet? A mutual friend introduced us and thought we would be good for each other.

My lesson: Three is a crowd! LOL

Guy 5

Let me introduce Trey. Trey was a former "Thugs-N-Harmony" kind of guy. He used to run the streets until God saved him. He was divorced and had a child. He was hot and heavy!

I had never dated a former thug before, and I am so thankful for the experience. He saw things from a different perspective, and I learned a lot from him. He had relocated to the area and I was open to being his Boo. It lasted about seven months. He soon stopped calling me, and started making excuses for not coming over. I knew those signs. He vanished without a trace.

About a year later, he called wanting to go out. When I asked him if he was dating someone else, he could not give me a straight answer. I told him not to call me anymore. He is now married, and, yes, he is still fine. Did I say that? Yep. Best wishes!

My lesson: Thug love can be addictive, but it is not always fruitful. It can seem fun, but can be a trick of the enemy.

Guy 6

Meet Demetrius. We never actually dated long term, but he was my best friend. We met through a relative who thought he was good for me. On the first date we knew we would not work as a couple, but we continued to communicate because we had good chemistry as friends.

He was real cool and stimulating. He was like the brother I had never had. We talked all the time. He kept it real 100 percent of the time, and I did the same. He would always tease me about being single, and I would always tease him about being married three times.

My lesson: Every person you meet and go on a date with will not lead to marriage. Enjoy the moment and the pleasure of good company. You may make a friend.

This list is only a few of the guys I have dated. I have learned so much from each person I have dated. The process was sometimes painful when it did not work out, but I had to learn to reflect, pull out some golden nuggets, and carry on. My dating experiences have helped shape and mold me into who I am today.

Everything I have acquired or accomplished has been a result of my walk of faith. Nothing was given to me on a silver platter. Am I grateful? Yep, all the time. Would I change anything? Nope, it made me who I am today.

I am who I am because of what I had, didn't have, and who I am in Christ. My ups and downs and hills and valleys all helped make me who I am today.

I take nothing for granted. From driving to the grocery store, to paying bills, to going to work or to church, to having a conversation with loved ones, to seeing a cute guy and flirting.

I do flirt sometimes (with single men only) and its quite fun! The synergy between men and women is something robots and technology can never conceptualize. Science can't capture a DNA sample of chemistry. It's how God almighty created us. We are different in so many ways, and yet perfect for one another.

I have not neglected putting myself out there to date and get to know people. I have stepped out of my comfort zone, and I have learned from every experience, but have I come out of singlehood? Nope, not yet. Will it happen? Yep, I believe it will. In the meantime, I'm going to enjoy my life!

Do not let anyone take away the delight of being single. Do not let anyone take your joy out of being single. Am I trying to trap you into remaining single forever? No, I am not, but until God brings you your spouse, you are single, and you might as well enjoy it!

There may be some married people who mean well, but are probably clueless about your journey of singlehood. Love them, appreciate them, and keep moving.

Most people in my circle were married by the age of 30. My circle of single friends really has diminished and decreased over the years. How do I feel when I hear another engagement announcement? Super excited! Am I lying? No, I am not. Every time someone I know becomes engaged or married, I rejoice and say a prayer for them in my private time. Every time a new relationship emerged, I would literally celebrate and send up a quick prayer for them.

Jealously does not live in my heart. Love and celebration of others' lives in my heart. Celebrating others is a concept I learned from Pastor Edward Tyrone Turner. (Shout out to you, Pastor Turner! You rock!)

Pastor Turner is big on mindset, kingdom principles, and empowering God's kingdom to manifest in our lives. I have taken hold of those principals and I am a better person for it. Although I have the same desire for marriage I have always had, my time for a relationship has not yet come.

We dress and adorn our outer body, and we should. We keep our temple clean, and we should. We watch what we eat and go to the gym, and we should. But what about our mindsets? I am telling you, working on a healthy mindset will change your image and view of life! Once I begin to do that, wow! Wow is all I can say! It works!

You must change your mindset. Your mindset matters. Changing your mindset will shift your mental capacity and emotional state to one of peace, stability, and contentment. Make it your purpose to maintain a healthy mindset.

Scripture Moment

A thief comes to steal and kill and destroy,
but I came to give life—life in all its fullness.
John 10:10 (NCV)

Ministry Moment

It's Time to UPgrade

We were created in the image of God. We came from the dust of the ground and the rib of Adam. God created the heavens and the earth. Then, He created man to subdue it, to take dominion over it, and rule it. In the beginning, God made something out of nothing, and that is what He does with us.

He fills us with His divine purpose. His purpose has vision, destiny, creativity, rulership, dominion, and identity. Our identity can never be mistaken because our Father has adopted us into His Royal Priesthood.

Read I Peter 2:9-10 and Ephesians 1:5-6.
What a celebration! We were created, adopted, and given benefits all at once!

We are God's vessels of honor, ambassadors of Christ, and we should position ourselves to receive and be all God has created us to be. Athletes position themselves to win, and that is what we have to do in this game of life. Until our inner man and our thought processes awaken, we shall and will remain stagnant. As the Word of God and positive affirmations arise in you, you will find that the Holy Spirit in you is mighty and can do the impossible!

We must realize that we are no longer slaves, but kings and queens, joint heirs of a promise that is bigger than us! God's promises give us an inheritance right to a life flowing with milk and honey. We can live in abundance in every area of our life!

R&B artist, songwriter, and producer, Beyoncé, penned a song titled, "Upgrade U" featured on her second studio album, B-Day, released in 2006. The concept of the song revolved around a woman offering luxuries to a man to upgrade his lifestyle. The chorus goes a little something like this:

Partner let me upgrade you
Flip a new page
Introduce you to some new things and Upgrade you
I can (up) I can (up)
Let me upgrade you
(Partner let me upgrade.)

The urban dictionary defines Upgrade as, "To make someone a better person. He or she will take you up to the next level."

Does that not sound a lot like what God does for us? Does that not sound like Jesus? Does that not sound like the Holy Ghost? Our Lord can take you to the next level, the next dimension. It's Time to UPgrade your soul!

Another online dictionary defines "upgrade" as, "To raise something to a higher standard, in particular improve by adding or replacing components." Synonyms of the word are: improve, update, make better, and reform.

Does that not sound like the Kingdom of God? Recognize who you are in the Spirit, and attain it in the natural. It's time to UPgrade!

Do you remember the Prophet Elisha in the Old Testament? A prophet is a seer, someone that "sees" and reveals what God has to say. A prophet is also a part of the fivefold ministry found in Ephesians 4:11-12. Some people do not believe in prophets and feel that God will speak directly to them and not use anyone else. But Dr. Whirl wants you to know sometimes we are not in a position to hear a Word from God.

Biblical history denotes that the prophets Elijah and Elisha joined forces around I Kings, Chapter 19. Elijah was a mentor to Elisha. The prophet Elisha had received the mantle, a double portion of Elijah's spirit before he died. Guess what, Elisha didn't just happen to receive a double portion; he asked for it! *Read II King 2:9.*

Yes, Elijah opened his mouth and asked for a double portion. Receiving involves participation. Elisha was in position to receive. When Elijah died, Elisha became the main prophet on the scene and was already performing miracles by the Spirit of almighty God in Israel.

In the book of II Kings, God sent the prophet Elisha to the widow woman. Her husband had died, and she was desperate for assistance. The widow had a leftover bill from her husband that had gone into default. The creditors were blowing up her phone and email saying,

"Pay up or we can take your boys into custody for payment." In the Old Testament, at times poor people had to pay off debt by selling themselves or their children as slaves.

Elisha asked the widow a question in verse two. He said, "What do you have?"

She had something tucked away in her cabinet she was saving for a rainy day. She probably had forgotten about it. It's like that money you have stashed away for a new pair of earrings, or those silver dollars your relative gave you when you were a little child. She had the solution in her house, but could not see it due to her frustration and worry.

The widow woman had some oil; she didn't even realize God was in it. Guess what? God was waiting to come out. God was waiting to be activated.

I ask you the same question as you read this, what do you have? What talent do you have tucked away? What gift is lying dormant in your dreams at night? Release to God what you have hidden away!

What's in your house or in your hand that you cannot see due to anxiety? Sometimes we block ourselves from seeing what God has blessed us with. Life happens, and sometimes we need God to send us an angel. Be open to God doing something new in your life. He just may send a prophet your way!

Elisha had a double portion of God's Spirit on his life. The widow women had oil that God more than doubled! What blessing does God want to double in your life?

Our power can double in the spirit; we can do more in faith now than last year. Glory! That's good news. It's time to UPgrade!

There comes a time in your life when you've got to UPgrade. Come out of Babylon and live in the Kingdom with a divine agenda.

Where is the Kingdom of God? It is within. How do I access the Kingdom? Recognize who you are in Him.

There are three ways we can UPgrade and release what we have in our hands, allowing God to double it, or triple it, or more! Let's look at what the widow woman did, and follow her example.

1. She obeyed instruction.

God sent a prophet to UPgrade the widow woman. She surrendered what was in her hand when Elisha asked for it.

Who has God sent into your life to upgrade you? Who challenges you to push, keep moving, and do more? Who pushes you out of your comfort zone into your next level? Ask for their advice. Seek godly counsel and wisdom.

2. She did something different.

The widow woman was desperate. When you get sick and tired of being sick and tired, you will step out and do something different. Unveil where you are and push to accelerate yourself into your position in God's kingdom.

It could be something as simple as changing your diet, enrolling in a gym and working out, meeting new people, changing jobs, starting a new ministry at your church, or simply watching something different on TV.

The widow's husband had died. Her revenue stream had dried up, so she had to tap into different resources and flex muscles she did not know she had.

Sometimes God will remove your security blanket from around you, so you can take hold of His comfort blanket. That new boss, nosey neighbor, or aggravating church lady who always has a word for you could very well be the doorway God sent to help you to your breakthrough.

3. She was not afraid to seek help.

Superman and superwoman do not exist. Stop trying to be all you need. You and I are not enough. Think about God, when He put on flesh and walked this earth, He didn't do it alone. He added 12 disciples. He did not work in isolation. He surrounded himself with people who supported Him and followed His teachings. The 12 disciples tripled the work of the Father.

Jesus didn't work alone, and you and I cannot either. There are people on Earth who will help you and provide you with some form of assistance. God will direct you to those people, or He will bring them to you.

Okay. Now you know what to do. You know what is in your hand, and you know what God has created you for. Now, it's time to UPgrade! Do not be afraid!

UPgrade!

Pen Moment

Dating. Synergy. Upgrade.

As you reflect back on this chapter, let go of all past hurt, pain, and humiliation. Holding on to the pain and anger, is holding you hostage. What happened can not hurt you anymore. Wipe those tears and soar in victory.

For the next 5-7 days, channel your energy and reflect on every good thing that has happened. There is something good in everything you have experienced this far. Begin to thank God for everything you have gone through. As your words and thoughts change, your heart will become clean and whole again.

Prayer Moment

Lord, You are mighty. You are holy. You are supreme. I honor you as Lord and Ruler of my life.

I receive a mindset shift right now in Jesus' Name. May God give me joy that surpasses all understanding.

I ask You, Lord, to bind every demonic force that tries to shut me down mentally. I ask You, God, to command Your angels to surround me and give me a brand new thinking cap.

I put on the anointing of God. I receive a shift in my life; things are about to change for me. Complaining is about to cease and excellence is about to rise up in me.

No longer will I cry about why so-in-so left, or why he or she decided to marry someone else. I rejoice in advance that you have somebody better for me. Mantle of grace, mantle of new beginnings, mantle of favor, fall fresh on me now.

Amen.

Let the Healing Begin

Chapter 5

As a child, I stuttered a lot, so reading aloud in class was something I hated to do. I remember my classmates laughing at me from 1st grade to 12th grade. It hurt then, but I now walk in victory and can look back and smile.

I went to a speech therapist in grade school and even as an adult, but I felt calm with my therapist and I wouldn't stutter in front of her, so I stopped going. It wasn't until college that I was able to really work on my speech problem.

I often wondered why I had that trait. I researched and researched about it. I ended up deciding (this wasn't from the Lord) that if I didn't have a stutter there is no telling how many people I would have cussed out! So, I just didn't say anything. God has done a work in this Whirl! Praise Him!

I am an overcomer. There is nothing God can't do. I am here to tell you that whatever issue you are battling or facing, let God arise and every enemy be scattered!

May you be set free today in Jesus' Name! I been saved and sanctified a very long time, but God is still working on me. He still working on you too!

You don't have to be perfect when you meet your future love. No, you don't! Perfection does not exist, but some of your issues should be resolved. Don't be afraid to let your guard down and share what you still battle. Will we ever get it all together? No, not until heaven, but we can work on some issues. I've worked on a lot of my issues.

We all have issues that result from relational hurt through our process of singlehood and dating. When you bond with someone, they attach to you and you attach to them. The relationship becomes a part of your life. When that relationship is ripped away, it hurts, especially when our emotions were involved.

Singlehood is nothing to play around with. It is a very pivotal stage in our lives. During your single years, you can take control of your life and live life to the utmost, or you can let your difficult experiences take you out, and you can end up living beneath what God has for you.

After a relational loss, we are left with grief and brokenness. Sometimes our brokenness becomes so attached to us that it becomes a way of life and a part of our identity. We never detach from it. We wear our brokenness to church, work, and social events. Sometimes our brokenness causes us to miss out on life because we are so bitter.

We defend our broken places with the shield of, "That's just me," or "I just don't want to talk about it." At times, we push our pain so far back into our minds we don't even think about the parts of us that are broken. Sometimes we do not even acknowledge we need to be healed. We mask our pain and heartbreak very well, but, then, something triggers our silent alarms and we can't deny something isn't quite right.

As we grow in Christ and in this life, it is important for us to shed some things both physically and spiritually. Shedding means to rid oneself of something unwanted. As we grow and blossom, we need to make room for the new by shedding the old. In the physical, we shed dead skin cells, fingernails, and hair. In the spirit, we need to shed pain, disappointment, confusion, frustration, regret, and bitterness. Healing needs to take place before you say "I do." That is all I am trying to say. Don't take your hurt, pain, and dirt with you into a marriage.

Though we have been broken, God can put the pieces of our lives back together to form a more precious jewel than we started with. Sometimes God uses circumstances to break you, just so He can rebuild you for His purpose. He knows what He is doing. Even when we err, He looks at us and says, "She is going to get right back up!" He never gives up on us!

Once you have the strength to acknowledge the pain, healing can and will begin. Acknowledging pain allows God to step in. What hurt you? When did it hurt you? What changes have you made in your life, so you will not make the same decisions that hurt you again? What scriptures can you lean on to minister to your spirit?

Think about a garden. The gardener works the soil, plants the seed, waters it, and waits for growth. When harvest time comes, the gardener picks vegetables and fruit, and the whole process starts over again. The ground has to be tilled, cleaned, and fertilized.

That's how our lives are. God has to plow our hearts to prepare our ground to produce a harvest. He has to heal our land so that we can keep growing, growing, growing.

Healing is a process that involves death, burial, and resurrection. We have to shed the death of what hurt us. We have to bury what almost killed us. We have to be reborn through the resurrection power of Jesus Christ!

Don't take your past into your future unless it's as a testimony. Your future does not have room for your past. God designed our past to carry us into the now.

Scripture Moment

Beloved, I pray that you may prosper in all things
and be in health, just as your soul prospers.
3 John 2:1 (NKJV)

Ministry Moment
Rest in God

Have you ever had a season of life where you did not know what to do? I have. During that time, I turned to the wisdom of the Word and applied it to my life. Psalm 37:7 (KJV) says, "Rest in the LORD, and wait patiently for Him." Sometimes, resting in God is exactly what He wants us to do. When we are healing, we are required to rest. We can't heal properly if we do not rest.

The year 2015 was a year of rest for me. That year yielded a different flavor than I had experienced before. Many situations occurred that I had no solution for, and that I had to completely let go of. Circumstances evolved, and I did not know how to eradicate them. I had no answer. I had no resolution. Things I had prepared for failed. Things I had hoped for did not occur.

I had to completely let go of trying to find an answer—mentally, physically, and emotionally. I threw my hands up and said, "Okay! I am letting go of it and I am letting you, GOD, handle it." There were some things I had to walk away from and make up my mind to never look back. There were some obstacles I had to leave at the altar.

There were days when I would think about my situation and wonder, "What will my solution be?" Each time the question popped into my thoughts, I would say, "God, I trust You."

I had said, "God, I trust You" many times before, but this season was different. When I decided to let go, and I mean to really, really let go, I found a new place in God. I found a new place in the Comforter. I saw God in a different way, a better way. I began to adjust, refocus, and fine-tune my lens of philosophy. I begin to take a brand new journey of rest in Him.

I rested in God's detour and put my GPS away. I took a seat in the place He prepared for me. I took a seat in the chair He designed just for me. The place was uncomfortable to my carnality, but my spirit was alive, rejuvenated, and ready for the plans God had for me.

I think we all have those moments when He does something unexpected for us and we are like, "Where did that come from?" God works in unexpected and unanticipated ways. Resting in God is nothing more than the authentic, true you, meeting the authentic, divine Creator face-to-face, and you resting in the awe of His splendor.

Resting in God does not mean throwing in the towel. It means we allow God to call the shots. It means God is orchestrating the fiesta of our life. I had to get out of God's way and allow Him to be my Advocate. I had to allow Him to really work on my behalf. And now, I challenge you to get out of God's way, and let Him work on your behalf.

Daniel had to rest in God inside of the lion's den. Jacob had to rest in God as he sat wrongfully in prison. None of it made sense, but God allowed the situations to happen for a purpose. God purposely allows the enemy set us up to receive God's blessing and promotion.

During my uncomfortable year, 2015, I was where I needed to be, and I learned three things:

God's plan is always better.
God's route is always safer.
God's direction always leads to the solution I need.

The dictionary definition of rest is, "peace of mind and spirit, free of anxiety, something used for support." There are over 100 scriptures on rest in the Holy Bible.

When God's Word amplifies a concept, or repeats it several times, it is a sign that we must pay attention to what He is saying. Resting in God does not mean that we stop fighting the good fight of faith, or that we allow the enemy to take charge. Resting in God means that we allow God to take the lead and we follow. It means we allow Him to take the wheel and allow His perfect work to begin in our lives.

President Barack Obama had to rest in God when it looked like he had lost the presidential election. Dr. Martin Luther King, Jr. had to rest in God when his back was up against the wall. He knew the day of freedom and equality for all citizens and ethnicities would come—even if he did not live to see it. No, it's not a perfect world, but we are free in Christ.

God's plan is always better.
God's route is always safer.
God's direction always leads to the solution I need.

Those of us who have tapped into our kingdom authority understand and realize that God's plan is always better. God's route is always safer. God's direction always leads to the solution we need. Resting in God began to open my heart and my spirit to Him. Yes, I was already saved, but this experience of rest and trust was deeper. It went into the marrow of my bones. It filtered through my spirit. It awakened me to a new and profound look at life.

The book of Psalms is a place where we can find scriptures to connect to any circumstance or obstacle we face. Climbing mountainous circumstances help us build spiritual muscles of faith to carry out God's given assignment for our lives.

God is all we need. He has all the capability to work a good work in us. He is Lord, and we must rest while He completes His creative plan in our lives.

David authored many of the Psalms. Psalms are songs, poetry, and spontaneous prayers with a heavenly sound, which exalts our God and King. David and others wrote out their feelings during trials and wrote about the faith they held to: the Redeemer lives and works on their behalf. The theme of rest and trust flow throughout the Psalms.

Here are five reasons we must find rest in God:

1. His timing is perfect.

Trust his timing. God works from the end to the beginning. His work is finished. It is done. We are His creation, His ambassadors, His royal priesthood. We live the script, but He holds the copyright.

Read Isaiah 46:10.

God's plan is always better. God's route is always safer. God's direction always leads to the solution I need.

2. He is Lord.

Trust His Lordship. God is the Ruler. He is Master. He is King. He has the very last say. He has the final authority. We must surrender to the Highest Power, God.

Read Romans 14:11.

God's plan is always better. God's route is always safer. God's direction always leads to the solution I need.

3. He makes the best decisions for your life.

Trust His decisions for your life. If you are drawing a map for your life, make sure it lines up with His destiny for you. If your map does not match His map, you are in trouble.

Read Jeremiah 29:11.

God's plan is always better. God's route is always safer. God's direction always leads to the solution I need.

4. He has the right direction for your life.

Trusting His direction requires nothing but faith. Peter had the faith to walk on water. We too must focus on God and allow Him to lead us. Allow God to order your steps. Walk in His footprints. Totally surrender to His will and way.

God's plan is always better. God's route is always safer. God's direction always leads to the solution I need.

5. He has provided.

Trust His provision. There is no lack in God. His provisions will manifest as we trust beyond our fear.

Read Psalm 23:1.

God's plan is always better. God's route is always safer. God's direction always leads to the solution I need.

Pen Moment

At this time, I want you to write out some positive affirmations about you, and then speak them out loud.

Before you speak, I want you to believe everything that you are about to release into the atmosphere.

Remember that words have power. Death and Life are in the power of the tongue. I believe we literally set our course of life by what we say.

Are you ready? Let's do this. I will start, but you can finish.

I am somebody. I display the righteousness of God. I am more than a conqueror. I am healed. I am set free. I am redeemed by the Blood of the Lamb.

I hear clearly. I see clearly. I am wealthy. I am healthy. I am joyful. I receive all the promises of the Lord.

God has more for my life. The Greater One lives inside of me. I know my Redeemer live. I know there is more for me.

I won't let go of God. God is with me at all times. Angels surround me at all times. I walk in favor. I walk in prosperity. I live in full abundance.

I affirm today that my life is getting better. What used to bother me no longer has a hold on me What used to make me cry now gives me a confident smile.

Prayer Moment

As the deer pants after the water, my soul longs for You, Lord. That's how much I need You today.

Let the healing begin in me. From my past until now, I give You every inch of me that is both whole, and jacked up.

Clean me up. Heal me from the pain. Heal me from the shame. Take the pain away. Take the agony away.

Be healed all over. Be healed in the bones, blood, fibers, cells, mental state, and emotional capacity. I am more than a conqueror in Jesus.

When I let it go, and really let it go, that is when the healing will begin. I have carried this weight for quite sometime, but today, I want to give it to You.

As I give it to You, I may scream and I may cry, but Lord, You've got me. Don't let me go.

This pain has become a part of who I am, but today I give it to You. I trust that You will fill the void and I will hope again. I will love again. I will shine again.

I feel a release. I feel a weight being lifted. I feel Your presence. I know You are with me. This is my prayer.

Amen. I love You forever.

Your Price is Right!

Chapter 6

God created some people to be wives, and some to be husbands. He created other people to be single. Take some time to seek the Lord. Find His purpose for your life. It will mean surrendering to His purpose, even when His plan is not your desire. As you surrender your heart to the Lord, He will give you the desires He has for you.

There is nothing wrong with being single. There is nothing wrong with you. You are not too tall. You are not too short. You are not too thin. You are not too thick. Your hair is not too straight. Your hair is not too bushy. You are not too dark. You are not too light. Carmel and Chocolate both have a sweet taste!

There is nothing wrong with being single. There is nothing wrong with you. It is okay to wake up alone in bed. It's okay to go to a camp meeting revival solo. It is okay to go to a family dinner alone.

Strut your stuff; shake what your mama gave ya! That's what's up! Twerk if you can! Work with what you've got, so when your love comes you will be ready to work your life for real.

I cannot change your current situation. I cannot change your marital status whether you are single, separated, divorced, or widowed. But I can add value to your thought process. I can speak a word into your life about your worth. I can encourage you to change your thoughts, so you can elevate to success.

There is a monetary value associated with purchasing a home. You have to pay a price when you purchase a vehicle. Even our daily necessities, like food, cost us something. Everything in life that is needful, or a blessing, requires us to give in order to receive.

There is a value attached to your self-worth, your life, and you. Your value isn't a dollar amount; you are priceless. Your value doesn't register with the current market value. You are worth more than anything money can buy; that's why you are not for sale—not even to the highest bidder. You are reserved for a God ordained relationship that only God can arrange. The cost to love you is commitment—the whole of another person's heart, mind, and body—in covenant with you giving them the same respect.

Fix Up. Clean Up. Rise Up. Your price is right. Your pearls of wisdom are a royal collection. Your irresistible image is a charm. Your ego is not too boastful. Your price is right. It is right to wait for God's best plan for you.

Your season of singlehood will soon come to an end. Maximize every moment you have to work on you. Remember, singleness is a gift God gave you; it is a jewel. When the King gives you something, treasure it. Your gift of singleness can evolve you to a place where you will be able to reach your relational dreams. Your gift of singleness can develop you into a place where you can receive your promise. Most of all, your gift of singleness can advance you toward an eternal relationship with the Lord. God knows what you need; trust Him!

Scripture Moment

For we are God's masterpiece. He has created
us anew in Christ Jesus, so we can do the
good things He planned for us long ago.
Ephesians 2:10 (NLT)

Ministry Moment
Moving Forward with the Promise

In this season and time of life that we live in, it is essential that we move forward into all that God has in store for us! Time waits on no one. The clock ticks and tocks; the days pass by from Sunday to Saturday, and the 24 hours of the day continue to move.

Read Hebrews 10:35-36.

Nothing moves backwards. Everything that God is connected to moves forward. God is stable. He is consistent. He is the same yesterday, today, and forevermore. As the Amplified Bible says, God is eternally changeless. How many people can wear that title?

He is stable in His love and sovereignty. He is consistent in His global awareness of His creation, and He never changes. He lives in eternity, and we must grab hold to Him and move forward. He left us His Word, the Holy Bible. He left us a Comforter, the Holy Spirit.

Moving forward into the promises of God affords us the opportunity to behold all that God has in store for us. His promises connect us to our future. His promises connect us to our destiny. His promises comprise all of who He is and what He has for us. His promises are the same in the 21st Century despite social media, technology, and corporate America.

God is love. God is compassion. God is all and all. He is still Alpha and Omega. He still reigns. He still deserves the glory. He still wants us to follow him. He still wants us to preach the Gospel. Don't let life's busyness squeeze God out.

The Apostle Paul was tenacious. He took a lot of hits, but he knew how to move forward with God's promises. He knew he had to grab hold of God and move forward into what was ahead.

Read Philippians 3:12-14 in The Voice version of the Bible.

To move forward in this season, you have to grab hold of God's Word! God's Word is still relevant in today's age. There would be no New Testament without the Old Testament. The Old Testament is the foundation that prepares us for the New Testament and Jesus Christ!

Without the law, we would not understand our need for a sacrificial Savior. We are living under grace by the blood Jesus shed! Stop trying to be the law, and let God arise in your life! The law shows us our sin, but Jesus shows us the way forward!

Some of us are stuck in what happened and can't see what is ahead. The past happened, and it isn't coming back. It happened, and you learned from it. It happened, and you survived. God is present. He is not in the past. He does something new every day. We must move forward with Him. If we move opposite of Him, we become stagnant and stale. Move forward with His promise.

The word "move" is defined as: to take action; to advance or progress; to promote. Does that not sound like God? He moves us forward with progress and promotion to advance the kingdom.

Read I Corinthians 15:58, Romans 8:37, and Psalm 75:6-7.

The word "promise" is defined as: a statement telling someone that you will definitely do something in the future; an indication of future success; a reason to expect that something will happen in the future.

Read Ephesians 3:20.

The word "forward" is defined as: toward the future, to help make progress, or getting ready for the future.

Read Isaiah 46:10.

God is connected to His promises. The promises are connected to God. He has already prepared His promises for us. Remember, God is eternal, and He is eternally changeless.

The book of Hebrews discusses the new kingdom of God. The new kingdom of God represents the New Testament, under the covering of the blood of the Lamb. We won't fully enter into the totality of Kingdom until we transition to Heaven, but there are some perks we can embrace while we are here on Earth!

The new Kingdom of God embodies Jesus Christ as the High Priest. The book of Hebrews compares the Old Testament sacrificial offerings to the sacrifice of Jesus. Old Testament High Priests could not save us; their duties brought justice for a moment, but people needed a Savior.

The book of Hebrews is well known for discussing faith in Chapter 11. It is a rich book, filled with the glories of who God is, and what He means in our lives.

Jesus Christ became our final and ultimate High Priest. A High Priest represents the people before God, and that is what Jesus Christ does for us. He intercedes on our behalf. He pleads our case before the Father. He is the best lawyer anybody could have.

Read Hebrews 1:3, Hebrews 2:14, and Hebrews 9:13-15.

Hebrews 10 discusses how we may face ridicule and suffering for knowing Christ. The scriptures exhort us not to cast away our confidence. Things may not have gone according to our plans, but it is all working out for our good. God still has a reward for us. God will still keep His Word. He has so much in store for us.

Focus more on Him, and less on your insufficiencies. Focus more on the promise, and less on what you didn't get right, or can't get right.

How do I move forward?

Move. You must move to obtain the promise.
Plant. You plant before you reap.
Harvest. You must reap and anticipate a harvest.
Stop looking back!

Jesus died on the cross and He resurrected from the dead! Thank God for what He did! God wants us to move forward with His legacy of defeating and conquering death. We rest in His life, but that doesn't mean we become stagnated. His death, resurrection, and teachings advance us into the next generation. We must take hold of His promises through service, evangelism, and love.

Don't let ancestors or traditions hold you hostage.

Read Mark 7:13.
It is okay to step out of the box into God's promise with His Word! Look at those who have stepped out: Tyler Perry, Oprah Winfrey, and Dublin City Police Chief, Bishop Tim Chatman! They each held to the promise of their faith and moved forward with that promise in mind! We must move forward with God's promise in mind!

Pen Moment

Well, you made it to the end of this book. That signifies that you can make it in this life. You just witnessed a sniped written reality of my life for the past 20 years.

What can I say!? God has proven Himself to me over and over. As I look back, I would not change a thing.

My deepest prayer is that you surrender any fear or withdrawal you are experiencing in your life right now.

You must realize and know there is nothing wrong with being single. Let nobody make you feel little or insignificant because your boyfriend has not proposed or you have not had a date in a while. So what?

Some people rush God! But God moves at His own speed. He is never late. Learn to go high when they go low. Alright! I borrowed that from Michelle Obama!

Appreciate you! I love you! Go to the next level!

If you don't appreciate you, he or she won't either. Again, I can not tell you how to find him or her, because this is not a dating book. I do have a right to tell you. It's okay to be single.

Enjoy and appreciate your gift. When you least expect, a relationship in God's plan will happen for you.

Take that pen and discover you. Start a journal to track God's goodness in your life. Commit to writing about how He is using your singlehood for His plan.

Prayer Moment

Lord God,

You are good and Your mercies endure forever. You are great and Your mercies endure for ever.

I am Your masterpiece, created to give You glory and to be all that You made me to be. Take me as I am and work on me. I am not perfect, but I am Yours. I have issues, but I am Yours.

I am willing to let go so You can shower me with Your promises. I am ready to receive. I am ready to let go of my past.

I am apart of Your chosen generation and Your royal priesthood. I am valuable and deserve Your best. Doors closed so others could open. People walked away so I could make progress on my journey. People came so I could become stronger and better.

Bitterness and sour lemons have no place in me. I let go of it all. Your price is right just for me! At Your command and through Your word, release Your promises into me.

I speak victory into the atmosphere, and I know Your word will not return void. You are a on-time God.

I love You forever!

Amen!

About the Author

    Yasmin Whirl is a native of Toomsboro, Georgia, and the oldest of three daughters of Willie C. and Irene Strange. She currently resides in Dublin, Georgia.

    At an early age, Minister Whirl knew God had something special for her to do. Upon going to college in 1993, she gave her life to Jesus Christ at the age of 18. She gives glory to Almighty God for the men and women who have shaped her path.

She served for over 20 years under Rev. Arthur L. Gordon III, at Jordan Stream Baptist Church. God then shifted her to Discipleship Christian Center Church, where she served faithfully for 5 years under Bishop Gus H. Copper. She was licensed into the ministry in 2009.

She has served the past 11 years at Kingdom Living Church under Pastor Edward Tyrone Turner.

She works full time for the Wilkinson County Board of Education as a High School Counselor, and has worked in public education for 20 years.

She holds a Doctorate and Specialist Degree in Educational Leadership, a Specialist and Master's Degree in Counseling, and a Bachelor's Degree in Sociology.

She is a proud member of Alpha Kappa Alpha Sorority, Inc. She is currently attending seminary school at Interdenominational Theological Center in Atlanta, Georgia.

Follow Yasmin Whirl on social media:

Twitter @ywhirl
Instagram @ywhirl
Facebook Yasmin Whirl

Our Written Lives
Christian Publishing
www.OurWrittenLives.com